Baby Bat's Lullaby

For Syd, my baby bat

—J.M.

For Clyde Bulla

—J.N.

ISBN 0-439-90088-3

Text copyright © 2004 by Jacquelyn Mitchard.
Illustrations copyright © 2004 by Julia Noonan. All rights reserved.
Published by Scholastic Inc., 557 Broadway, New York, NY 10012,
by arrangement with HarperCollins Publishers. SCHOLASTIC
and associated logos are trademarks and/or registered trademarks
of Scholastic Inc.

12 11 10 9 8 7 6 5 4 3 2 1   6 7 8 9 10 11/0

Printed in the U.S.A.   40

This edition first printing, September 2006

The art was made with acrylic and oil paints on paper.
Typography by Elynn Cohen

JACQUELYN MITCHARD

Baby Bat's Lullaby

illustrated by JULIA NOONAN

SCHOLASTIC INC.
New York Toronto London Auckland Sydney
Mexico City New Delhi Hong Kong Buenos Aires

Go to sleep,
Small new prince of the dark,
Quick dancer in the sky park,

Field squeaker,
Forest streaker,

Little wings petal-light,
Little teeth sugar-white.

My darling night creeper,
All-morning sleeper,
My baby bat.

Go to sleep,
Barn-hall glider,
Twilight slider,

Mosquito frightening,
Swift as lightning,

Dearer than night,
Brown eyes bright,

My jewel so soft,
My dancer aloft,
My baby bat.

Sleep beside me,
Master flyer,

Upside-down clinger,
Little-toe swinger,

Wings wrapped tight,
Cuddle till night.

Under Mama's soft gaze
Dream away dozy days,
For at dusk we shall play.

Strong little sweetling,
Mama's best treatling,

Sleep, little
Fleet little
Dear baby bat.